W. E. Gladstone

**A Chapter of Autobiography**

W. E. Gladstone

**A Chapter of Autobiography**

ISBN/EAN: 9783337012229

Printed in Europe, USA, Canada, Australia, Japan

Cover: Foto ©Raphael Reischuk / pixelio.de

More available books at **www.hansebooks.com**

A

# CHAPTER OF AUTOBIOGRAPHY.

BY

## THE RIGHT HON. W. E. GLADSTONE.

" Blame not, before thou hast examined the truth : understand
first, and then rebuke."—ECCLESIASTICUS, ch. ii.

LONDON:

JOHN MURRAY, ALBEMARLE STREET.

1868.

LONDON: PRINTED BY WILLIAM CLOWES AND SONS, DUKE STREET, STAMFORD STREET,
AND CHARING CROSS.

# INTRODUCTION.

At a time when the Established Church of Ireland is on her trial, it is not unfair that her assailants should be placed upon their trial too : most of all, if they have at one time been her sanguine defenders.

But if not the matter of the indictment against them, at any rate that of their defence, should be kept apart, as far as they are concerned, from the public controversy, that it may not darken or perplex the greater issue.

It is in the character of the author of a book called 'The State in its Relations with the Church,' that I offer these pages to those who may feel a disposition to examine them. They were written at the date attached to them; but their publication has been delayed until after the stress of the General Election.

# CHAPTER OF AUTOBIOGRAPHY.

AUTOBIOGRAPHY is commonly interesting ; but there can, I suppose, be little doubt that, as a general rule, it should be posthumous. The close of an active career supplies an obvious exception : for this resembles the gentle death which, according to ancient fable, was rather imparted than inflicted by the tender arrows of Apollo and of Artemis. I have asked myself many times, during the present year, whether peculiar combinations of circumstance might not also afford a warrant at times for departure from the general rule, so far as some special passage of life is concerned ; and whether I was not myself now placed in one of those special combinations.

The motives, which incline me to answer these questions in the affirmative, are mainly two. First, that the great and glaring change in my course of action with respect to the Established Church of Ireland is not the mere eccentricity, or even perversion, of an individual mind, but connects itself with silent changes, which are advancing in the very bed and basis of modern society. Secondly, that the progress of a great cause, signal as it has been and is, appears liable nevertheless to suffer in point of credit, if not of energy and rapidity, from the real or supposed delinquencies of a person, with whose name for the moment it happens to be specially associated.

One thing is clear : that if I am warranted in treating my own case as an excepted case, I am bound so to treat it. It is only with a view to the promotion of some general interest, that the public can becomingly be invited to hear more, especially in personal history, about an individual, of whom they already hear too much. But if it be for the general interest to relieve 'an enterprise of pith and moment' from the odium of baseness, and from the lighter reproach of precipitancy, I must make the attempt; though the obtrusion of the first person, and of all that it carries in its train, must be irksome alike to the reader and the writer.

So far, indeed, as my observation has gone, the Liberal party of this country have stood fire unflinchingly under the heavy vollies which have been fired into its camp with ammunition that had been drawn from depositories full only with matter personal to myself. And, with the confidence they entertain in the justice and wisdom of the policy they recommend, it would have been weak and childish to act otherwise. Still, I should be glad to give them the means of knowing that the case may not after all be so scandalous as they are told. In the year 1827, if I remember right, when Mr. Canning had just become Prime Minister, an effort was made to support him in the town of Liverpool, where the light and music of his eloquence had not yet died away, by an Address to the Crown. The proposal was supported by an able and cultivated Unitarian Minister, Mr. Shepherd, who had been one of Mr. Canning's opponents at former periods in the Liverpool elections. Vindicating the consistency of his course, he said he was ready to support the devil himself, if it had been necessary, in doing good. This was a succinct and rough manner of disposing of the question in the last resort. I hope, however, that those who sustain the Liberal policy respecting the Established Church of Ireland, will not be driven to so dire an extremity. It can hardly be deemed on my part an unnatural desire, that political friends, and candid observers, should on grounds of reason and knowledge, and not merely from friendly prepossession, feel themselves warranted not to believe in the justice of language such as by way of example I subjoin. I must, however, suppose that the author of it is persuaded of its fairness and justice, since he bears Her Majesty's Commission ; and his statement is adopted and pub-lished by a brother-officer, who is himself a candidate for Berwick in the ministerial interest, and therefore (I presume) not particularly squeamish on the sub-ject of political consistency, although I entertain no doubt that both are gallant, upright, and estimable gentlemen.

" There is obviously no need, on the present occasion at least, to extend this catalogue of the political delinquencies of this would-be demagogue, whom we may accordingly leave gibbeted and swinging in the winds of the fools' paradise! an object of derision and contempt to those at least who maintain that integrity of purpose and consistency ought not altogether to be discarded from public life."*

It freezes the blood, in moments of retirement and reflexion, for a man to think that he can have pre-

* From a placard just published at Berwick.

sented a picture so hideous to the view of a fellow-creature!

One thing I have not done, and shall not do. I shall not attempt to laugh off the question, or to attenuate its importance. In theory at least, and for others, I am myself a purist with respect to what touches the consistency of statesmen. Change of opinion, in those to whose judgment the public looks more or less to assist its own, is an evil to the country, although a much smaller evil than their persistence in a course which they know to be wrong. It is not always to be blamed. But it is always to be watched with vigilance; always to be challenged, and put upon its trial. The question is one of so much interest, that it may justify a few remarks.

It can hardly escape even cursory observation, that the present century has seen a great increase in the instances of what is called political inconsistency. It is needless, and it would be invidious, to refer to names. Among the living, however, who have occupied leading positions, and among the dead of the last twenty years, numerous instances will at once occur to the mind, of men who have been constrained to abandon in middle and mature, or even in advanced life, convictions which they had cherished through long years of conflict and vicissitude : and of men, too, who have not been so fortunate as to close or continue their career in the same political connexion as that in which they commenced it. If we go a little farther back, to the day of Mr. Pitt and Mr. Fox, or even to the day of Mr. Canning, Lord Londonderry, or Lord Liverpool, we must be struck with the difference. A great political and social convulsion, like the French Revolution, of necessity deranged the ranks of party; yet not even then did any man of great name, or of a high order of mind, permanently change his side.

If we have witnessed in the last forty years, beginning with the epoch of Roman Catholic Emancipation, a great increase in the changes of party, or of opinion, among prominent men, we are not at once to leap to the conclusion that public character, as a rule, has been either less upright, or even less vigorous. The explanation is rather to be found in this, that the movement of the public mind has been of a nature entirely transcending former experience; and that it has likewise been more promptly and more effectively represented, than at any earlier period, in the action of the Government and the Legislature.

If it is the office of law and of institutions to reflect the wants and wishes of the country, (and its wishes must ever be a considerable element in its wants), then, as the nation passes from a stationary into a progressive period, it will justly require that the changes in its own condition and views should be represented in the professions and actions of its leading men. For they exist for its sake, not it for theirs. It remains indeed their business, now and ever, to take honour and duty for their guides, and not the mere demand or purpose of the passing hour; but honour and duty themselves require their loyal servant to take account of the state of facts in which he is to work, and, while ever labouring to elevate the standard of opinion and action around him, to remember that his business is not to construct, with self-chosen materials, an Utopia or a Republic of Plato, but to conduct the affairs of a living and working community of men, who have self-government recognised as in the last resort the moving spring of their political life, and of the institutions which are its outward vesture.

The gradual transfer of political power from groups and limited classes to the community, and the constant seething of the public mind, in fermentation upon a vast mass of moral and social, as well as merely political, interests, offer conditions of action, in which it is evident that the statesman, in order to preserve the same amount of consistency as his antecessors in other times, must be gifted with a far larger range of foresight. But Nature has endowed him with no such superiority. It may be true that Sir Robert Peel shewed this relative deficiency in foresight, with reference to Roman Catholic Emancipation, to Reform, and to the Corn Law. It does not follow that many, who have escaped the reproach, could have stood the trial. For them the barometer was less unsteady; the future less exacting in its demands. But let us suppose that we could secure this enlargement of onward view, this faculty of measuring and ascertaining to-day the wants of a remote hereafter, in our statesmen; we should not even then be at the end of our difficulties. For the public mind is to a great degree unconscious of its own progression; and it would resent and repudiate, if offered to its immature judgment, the very policy, which after a while it will gravely consider, and after another while enthusiastically embrace.

Yet, as it still remains true that the actual opinions and professions of men in office, and men in authority without office, are among the main landmarks on which the public has to rely, it may seem that, in vindicating an apparent liberty of change, we destroy the principal guarantees of integrity which are available for the nation at large, and with these all its confidence in the persons who are to manage its affairs. This would be a consequence so fatal, that it might even drive us back upon the hopeless attempt to stereotype the minds of men, and fasten on their manhood the swaddling clothes of their infancy. But such is not the alternative. We may regulate the changes which we cannot forbid, by subjecting them to the test of public scrutiny, and by directing that scrutiny to the enforcement of the laws of moral obligation. There are abundant signs, by which to distinguish between those changes, which prove nothing worse than the fallibility of the individual mind, and manœuvres which destroy confidence, and entail merited dishonour. Changes which are sudden and precipitate—changes accompanied with a light and contemptuous repudiation of the former self— changes which are systematically timed and tuned to the interest of personal advancement—changes which are hooded, slurred over, or denied—for these changes, and such as these, I have not one word to say ; and if they can be justly charged upon me, I can no longer desire that any portion, however small, of the concerns or interests of my countrymen should be lodged in my hands.

Let me now endeavour to state the offence of which I am held guilty. *Ille ego qui quondam :* I, the person who have now accepted a foremost share of the responsibility of endeavouring to put an end to the existence of the Irish Church as an Establish-

ment, am also the person who, of all men in official,
perhaps in public life, did, until the year 1841,
recommend, upon the highest and most imperious
grounds, its resolute maintenance.

The book entitled ' The State in its Relations with
the Church' was printed during the autumn of 1838,
while I was making a tour in the South of Europe,
which the state of my eyesight had rendered it
prudent to undertake.    Three editions of it were
published without textual change; and in the year
1841 a fourth, greatly enlarged, though in other
respects little altered, issued from the press.    All
interest in it had, however, even at that time, long
gone by, and it lived for nearly thirty years only in
the vigorous and brilliant, though not (in my opinion)
entirely faithful picture, drawn by the accomplished
hand of Lord Macaulay.    During the present year,
as I understand from good authority, it has again
been in demand, and in my hearing it has received
the emphatic suffrages of many, of whose approval I
was never made aware during the earlier and less
noisy stages of its existence.

The distinctive principle of the book was supposed
to be, that the State had a conscience.    But the controversy really lies not in the existence of a conscience
in the State, so much as in the extent of its range.
Few would deny the obligation of a State to follow
the moral law.    Every Treaty, for example, proceeds
upon it.    The true issue was this : whether the State,
in its best condition, has such a conscience as can
take cognizance of religious truth and error, and in
particular whether the State of the United Kingdom,
at a period somewhat exceeding thirty years ago, was

or was not so far in that condition as to be under an obligation to give an active and an exclusive support to the established religion of the country.

The work attempted to survey the actual state of the relations between the State and the Church ; to show from History the ground which had been defined for the National Church at the Reformation ; and to inquire and determine whether the existing state of things was worth preserving, and defending against encroachment from whatever quarter. This question it decided emphatically in the affirmative.

An early copy of the Review containing the powerful essay of Lord Macaulay was sent to me ; and I found that to the main proposition, sufficiently startling, of the work itself, the reviewer had added this assumption, that it contemplated not indeed per-secution, but yet the retrogressive process of disabling and disqualifying from civil office all those who did not adhere to the religion of the State. Before (I think) the number of the ' Edinburgh Review ' for April, 1839, could have been in the hands of the public, I had addressed to Lord (then Mr.) Macaulay the following letter, which I shall make no apology for inserting, inasmuch as it will introduce one more morsel of his writing, for which the public justly shows a keen and insatiable appetite.

DEAR SIR,                    6, Carlton Gardens, April 10th, 1839.

I have been favoured with a copy of the forthcoming number of the 'Edinburgh Review,' and I perhaps too much presume upon the bare acquaintance with you of which alone I can boast, in thus unceremoniously assuming you to be the author of the article entitled ' Church and State,' and in offering you my very warm and cordial thanks for the manner in which you have treated both the work, and the author, on whom you deigned to bestow your attention. In whatever you write, you can hardly hope for the privilege of most anonymous productions, a real concealment; but if it had been possible not to recognize you, I should have questioned your authorship in this particular case, because the candour and single-mindedness which it exhibits are, in one who has long been connected in the most distinguished manner with political party, so rare as to be almost incredible.

I hope to derive material benefit, at some more tranquil season, from a consideration of your argument throughout. I am painfully sensible, whenever I have occasion to re-open the book, of its shortcomings, not only of the subject but even of my own conceptions : and I am led to suspect that, under the influence of most kindly feelings, you have omitted to criticize many things besides the argument, which might fairly have come within your animadversion.

In the mean time I hope you will allow me to apprise you that on one material point especially I am not so far removed from you as you suppose. I am not conscious that I have said either that the *Test Act* should be repealed, or that it should not have been passed : and though on such subjects language has many bearings which escape the view of the writer at the moment when the pen is in his hand, yet I think that I can hardly have put forth either of these propositions, because I have never entertained the corresponding sentiments. Undoubtedly I should speak of the pure abstract idea of Church and State as implying that they are co-extensive : and I should regard the present composition of the State of the United Kingdom as a deviation from that pure idea, but only in the same sense as all differences of religious opinion in the Church are a deviation from its pure idea, while I not only allow that they are permitted, but believe that (within limits) they were intended to be permitted. There are some of these deflections from abstract theory which appear to me allowable; and that of the admission of persons not holding the national creed into civil office is one which, in my view, must be determined by times and circumstances. At the same time I do not recede from any protest which I have made against the principle, that religious differences are irrelevant to the question of competency for civil office: but I would take my stand between the opposite extremes, the one that no such differences are to be taken into view, the other that all such differences are to constitute disqualifications.

I need hardly say the question I raise is not whether you have misrepresented me, for, were I disposed to anything so weak, the whole internal evidence and clear intention of your article would confute me : indeed I feel I ought to apologize for even supposing that you may have been mistaken in the apprehension of my meaning, and I freely admit on the other hand the possibility that, totally without my own knowledge, my language may have led to such an interpretation.

In these lacerating times one clings to everything of personal kindness in the past, to husband it for the future, and if you will allow me I shall earnestly desire to carry with me such a recollection of your mode of dealing with the subject; upon which, the attainment of truth, we shall agree, so materially depends upon the temper in which the search for it is instituted and conducted.

I did not mean to have troubled you at so much length, and I have only to add that I am, with much respect,

Dear Sir,

Very truly yours,

W. E. GLADSTONE.

T. B. MACAULAY, ESQ.

---

MY DEAR SIR,                              3, Clarges Street, April 11th, 1839.

I have very seldom been more gratified than by the very kind note which I have just received from you. Your book itself, and everything that I heard about you, though almost all my information came—to the honour, I must say, of our troubled times—from people very strongly opposed to you in politics, led me to regard you with respect and good will,

C

and I am truly glad that I have succeeded in marking those
feelings. I was half afraid when I read myself over again
in print, that the button, as is too common in controversial
fencing even between friends, had once or twice come off
the foil.

I am very glad to find that we do not differ so widely as I
had apprehended about the Test Act. I can easily explain
the way in which I was misled. Your general principle is
that religious non-conformity ought to be a disqualification
for civil office. In page 238 you say that the true and
authentic mode of ascertaining conformity is the Act of
Communion. I thought, therefore, that your theory pointed
directly to a renewal of the Test Act. And I do not recollect that you have ever used any expression importing
that your theory ought in practice to be modified by any
considerations of civil prudence. All the exceptions that you
mention are, as far as I remember, founded on positive
contract—not one on expediency, even in cases where the
expediency is so strong and so obvious that most statesmen
would call it necessity. If I had understood that you meant
your rules to be followed out in practice only so far as might
be consistent with the peace and good government of society,
I should certainly have expressed myself very differently in
several parts of my article.

Accept my warm thanks for your kindness, and believe me,
with every good wish,

My dear Sir,

Very truly yours,

T. B. MACAULAY.

W. E. GLADSTONE, ESQ., M.P.

Faithful to logic, and to its theory, my work did not
shrink from applying them to the crucial case of the
Irish Church. It did not disguise the difficulties of
the case, for I was alive to the paradox it involved.
But the one master idea of the system, that the State
as it then stood was capable in this age, as it had

been in ages long gone by, of assuming beneficially a responsibility for the inculcation of a particular religion, carried me through all. My doctrine was, that the Church, as established by law, was to be maintained for its truth; that this was the only principle on which it could be properly and permanently upheld; that this principle, if good in England, was good also for Ireland; that truth is of all possessions the most precious to the soul of man; and that to remove, as I then erroneously thought we should remove, this priceless treasure from the view and the reach of the Irish people, would be meanly to purchase their momentary favour at the expense of their permanent interests, and would be a high offence against our own sacred obligations.

These, I think, were the leading propositions of the work. In one important point, however, it was inconsistent with itself; it contained a full admission that a State might, by its nature and circumstances, be incapacitated from upholding and propagating a definite form of religion.*

"There may be a state of things in the United States of America, perhaps in some British colonies, there does actually exist a state of things, in which religious communions are so equally divided, or so variously subdivided, that the Government is itself similarly chequered in its religious complexion, and thus internally incapacitated by disunion from acting in matters of religion; or, again, there may be a State in which the members of Government may be of one faith or persuasion, the mass of the subjects of another, and hence there may be an external incapacity to act in matters of religion."

* 'The State in its Relations with the Church,' ch. ii., sect. 71, p. 73. Editions 1-3.

The book goes on to describe that incapacity, however produced, as a social defect and calamity. But the latter part of the work, instead of acknowledging such incapacity as a sufficient and indeed commanding plea for abstention, went beyond the bounds of moderation, and treated it as if it must in all cases be a sin; as though any association of men, in civil government or otherwise, could be responsible for acting beyond the line of the capabilities determined for it by its constitution and composition. My meaning I believe was, to describe only cases in which there might be a deliberate renunciation of such duties as there was the power to fulfil. But the line is left too obscurely drawn between this wilful and wanton rejection of opportunities for good, and the cases in which the state of religious convictions, together with the recognised principles of government, disable the civil power from including within its work the business of either directly or indirectly inculcating religion, and mark out for it a different line of action.

I believe that the foregoing passages describe fairly, if succinctly, the main propositions of ' The State in its Relations with the Church ; ' so far as the book bears upon the present controversy. They bound me hand and foot : they hemmed me in on every side. Further on I shall endeavour to indicate more clearly in what I think the book was right, and in what it was wrong. What I have now to show is the manner in which I retreated from an untenable position. To this retreat, and the time and mode of it, I now draw attention, and I will endeavour to apply to them the tests I have already laid down :—Was it sudden ?

Was it performed with an indecent levity? Was it made to minister to the interests of political ambition? Was the gravity of the case denied or understated? Was it daringly pretended that there had been no real change of front; and that, if the world had understood me otherwise, it had misunderstood me? My opinion of the Established Church of Ireland now is the direct opposite of what it was then. I then thought it reconcilable with civil and national justice; I now think the maintenance of it grossly unjust. I then thought its action was favourable to the interests of the religion which it teaches; I now believe it to be opposed to them.

But I must venture to point out that, whatever be the sharpness of this contradiction, it is one from which I could not possibly escape by endeavouring to maintain the Established Church of Ireland on the principles on which it is now maintained. I challenge all my censors to impugn me when I affirm that, if the propositions of my work are in conflict (as they are) with an assault upon the existence of the Irish Establishment, they are at least as much, or even more, hostile to the grounds on which it is now attempted to maintain it. At no time of my life did I propound the maxim *simpliciter* that we were to maintain the Establishment. I appeal to the few who may have examined my work otherwise than for the purpose of culling from it passages which would tell in a quotation. I appeal to the famous article of Lord Macaulay,* who says with truth—

" Mr. Gladstone's whole theory rests on this great fundamental proposition, that the propagation of re-

* ' Edinburgh Review,' April, 1839, p. 235.

ligious truth is one of the principal ends of government, as government. If Mr. Gladstone has not
proved this proposition, *his system vanishes at once.*"

This was entirely just. In the protest I addressed
to the distinguished Reviewer on a particular point, I
took no exception to it whatever. My work had
used (as far as I believe and remember) none of
the stock arguments for maintaining the Church of
Ireland. I did not say "maintain it, lest you should
disturb the settlement of property." I did not say
"maintain it, lest you should be driven to repeal the
Union." I did not say "maintain it, lest you should
offend and exasperate the Protestants." I did not
say "maintain it, because the body known as the
Irish Church has an indefeasible title to its property."
I did not say "maintain it for the spiritual benefit of
a small minority." Least of all did I say "maintain
it, but establish religious equality, setting up at the
public charge other establishments along with it, or
by distributing a sop here and a sop there, to coax
Roman Catholics and Presbyterians into a sort of
acquiescence in its being maintained." These topics
I never had made my own. Scarcely ever, in the
first efforts of debate, had I referred to one of them.
My trumpet, however shrill and feeble, had at least
rung out its note clearly. And my ground, right or
wrong it matters not for the present purpose, was
this : the Church of Ireland must be maintained for
the benefit of the whole people of Ireland, and must
be maintained as the truth, or it cannot be maintained at all.

Accordingly my book contended that the principle
of the Grant to Maynooth, unless as a simply cove-

nanted obligation,* and that of the Established Church of Ireland, could not stand together. In the House of Commons, on the question relating to the Grant, I am reported as having said in the year 1838,† that I objected to the Grant because it was fatal to the main principle on which the Established Church was founded.

And further. The Liberal Government and party of that day proposed, in 1835 and the following years, the famous "Appropriation Clause." The principle of their measure was, that the surplus funds only of the Irish Church were to be applied to popular education, after adequate provision had been made for the spiritual wants of the Protestants. This principle, that adequate provision is to be made for the spiritual wants of the Protestants, before any other claim on the property of the Irish Church can be admitted, was the basis of the Appropriation Clause; and is, as I understand the matter, the very principle which is now maintained against the Liberal party of 1868, by the (so-called) defenders of the Irish Established Church. But this principle I denounced in 1836 as strongly as I could now do. I extract the following passage from a report in 'Hansard,' which, as I remember, I had myself corrected, of a speech on the Irish Tithe Bill with the Appropriation Clause :—‡

"A Church Establishment is maintained either for the sake of its members or its doctrines; for those whom it

* p. 252.

† 'Mirror of Parliament,' Monday, July 30, 1838. The passage, which is full and clear, is more briefly given, but to the same effect, in 'Hansard,' vol. xliv. p. 817.

‡ June 1, 1836. 'Hansard,' vol. xxxiii. p. 1317.

teaches, or for that which it teaches.   On the former ground
it is not in equity tenable for a moment.

"Why should any preference be given to me over another
fellow-subject, or what claim have I personally to have my
religion supported, whilst another is disavowed by the State?
No claim whatever in respect to myself.   I concur entirely
with gentlemen opposite, hostile to an Establishment, that
no personal privilege ought in such a matter to be allowed.

"But if, on the contrary, I believe, as the great bulk of the
British Legislature does believe, that the doctrine and system
of the Establishment contain and exhibit truth in its purest
and most effective form, and if we also believe truth to be
good for the people universally, then we have a distinct and
immovable ground for the maintenance of an Establishment; but it follows as a matter of course from the principle,
that it must be maintained, not on a scale exactly and strictly
adjusted to the present number of its own members, but on
such a scale that it may also have the means of offering to
others the benefits which it habitually administers to them.

"Therefore we wish to see the Establishment in Ireland
upheld; not for the sake of the Protestants, but of the people
at large, that the ministers may be enabled to use the influences of their station, of kindly offices and neighbourhood, of
the various occasions which the daily intercourse and habits
of social life present; aye, and I do not hesitate to add of
persuasion itself, applied with a zeal tempered by knowledge
and discretion, in the propagation of that which is true, and
which, being true, is good as well for those who as yet have
it not, as well for those who have it.   It is the proposition of
the noble Lord which is really open to the charge of bigotry,
intolerance, and arbitrary selection; because, disavowing the
maintenance and extension of truth, he continues by way of
personal privilege to the Protestants the legal recognition of
their Church, which he refuses to the Church of the Roman
Catholic."

The negative part of this passage I adopt, except the
censure it implies upon Earl Russell and his friends;
who, whether their actual propositions were defensible

or not, had the "root of the matter" in their hearts, and were far ahead of me in their political forethought, and in their desire to hold up at least the banner of a generous and a hopeful policy towards Ireland.

In this manner I prove that, while I was bound by the propositions of my work, I was not singly but doubly bound. I was bound to defend the Irish Church, as long as it could be defended on the ground of its truth. But when the day arrived on which that ground was definitively abandoned, on which a policy was to be adopted by the Imperial Parliament such as to destroy this plea for the Irish Establishment, I was equally bound in such case to adopt no other : I had shown that justice would fail to warrant the mere support of the Church of the minority ; I was held, therefore, not to construct out of rags and tatters, shreds and patches, a new and different case for maintaining it on the ground of favour, or, as it is termed, justice, to Protestants ; and, if I had done anything of this kind, I should not have escaped the responsibility of inconsistency, but should simply have added a second and (as I think) a less excusable inconsistency to the first.

The day for the adoption of such a policy as I have described was not far distant.

Scarcely had my work issued from the press when I became aware that there was no party, no section of a party, no individual person probably in the House of Commons, who was prepared to act upon it. I found myself the last man on the sinking ship. Exclusive support to the established religion of the country, with a limited and local exception for Scotland under the Treaty of Union with that country, had been up to that time the actual rule of our policy; the instances to the contrary being of equivocal construction, and of infinitesimal amount. But the attempt to give this rule a vitality other than that of sufferance was an anachronism in time and in place. When I bid it live, it was just about to die. It was really a quickened and not a deadened conscience in the country, which insisted on enlarging the circle of State support, even while it tended to restrain the range of political interference in religion. The condition of our poor, of our criminals, of our military and naval services, and the backward state of popular education, forced on us a group of questions, before the moral pressure of which the old rules properly gave way. At and about the same period, new attempts to obtain grants of public money for the building of churches in England and Scotland, I am thankful to say, failed. The powerful Government of 1843 also failed to carry a measure of Factory Education, because of the preference it was thought to give to the Established Church. I believe the very first opinion I ever was called upon to give in Cabinet was an opinion in favour of the withdrawal of that measure.

In this state of facts and feelings, notwithstanding the strength of anti-Roman opinion, it was impossible that Ireland should not assert her share, and that a large one, to consideration in these critical matters. The forces, which were now at work, brought speedily to the front and to the top that question of Maynooth College, which I had always (rightly or wrongly) treated as a testing question for the foundations of the Irish Established Church; as, in point of principle, the *Articulus stantis aut cadentis Ecclesiæ.*

In the course of the year 1844, when I was a member of the Cabinet of Sir Robert Peel, he made known to me his opinion that it was desirable to remodel and to increase the Grant to Maynooth. I was the youngest member of that Government, entirely bound up with it in policy, and warmly attached, by respect and even affection, to its head and to some of its leading members. Of association with what was termed ultra-Toryism in general politics I had never dreamed. I well knew that the words of Sir R. Peel were not merely tentative, but that, as it was right they should, they indicated a fixed intention. The choice before me, therefore, was, to support his measure, or to retire from his Government into a position of complete isolation, and what was more than this, subject to a grave and general imputation of political eccentricity. My retirement, I knew, could have no other warrant than this : that it would be a tribute to those laws which, as I have urged, must be upheld for the restraint of changes of opinion and conduct in public men. For I never entertained the idea of opposing the measure of Sir Robert Peel. I can scarcely be guilty of a breach of confidence when I mention that Lord Derby, to whom I had already been indebted for much personal kindness, was one of those colleagues who sought to dissuade me from resigning my office. He urged upon me that such an act must be followed by resistance to the measure of the Government, and that I should run the risk of being mixed with a fierce religious agitation. I replied that I must adhere to my purpose of retirement, but that I did not perceive the necessity of its being followed by resistance to the proposal. Overtures were, not unnaturally, made to me by some of those who resisted it; but they were at once declined. My whole purpose was to place myself in a position in which I should be free to consider my course without being liable to any just suspicion on the ground of personal interest. It is not profane if I say "with a great price obtained I this freedom." The political association in which I stood was to me at the time the alpha and omega of public life. The Government of Sir Robert Peel was believed to be of immovable strength. My place, as President of the Board of Trade, was at the very kernel of its most interesting operations; for it was in progress from year to year, with continually waxing courage, towards the emancipation of industry, and therein towards the accomplishment of another great and blessed work of public justice. Giving up what I highly prized, aware that

. "malè sarta
Gratia nequicquam coit, et rescinditur,"*

I felt myself open to the charge of being opinionated, and wanting in deference to really great authorities; and I could not but know I should be regarded as fastidious and fanciful, fitter for a dreamer, or possibly a schoolman, than for the active purposes of public life in a busy and moving age. In effect so it was. In the month of January, 1845, if not sooner, the resolution of the Cabinet was taken; and I resigned. The public judgment, as might have been expected, did not favour the act. I remember that the ' Daily News,' then as now a journal greatly distinguished for an almost uniform impartiality, as well as for breadth

* Hor. Ep. ii. 3. 31.

of view and high discernment, remarked at the time
or afterwards upon the case, as a rare one, in which a
public man had injured himself with the public by an
act which must in fairness be taken to be an act of
self-denial. I hope that reference to this criticism will
not be considered boastful. It can hardly be so ; for an
infirm judgment, exhibited in a practical indiscretion,
is after all the theme of these pages. I do not claim
acquittal upon any one of the counts of indictment
which I have admitted may be brought against the
conduct I pursued. One point only I plead, and plead
with confidence. It proved that I was sensible of the
gravity of any great change in political conduct or
opinion, and desirous beyond all things of giving to
the country such guarantees as I could give of my
integrity, even at the expense of my judgment and
fitness for affairs. If any man doubts this, I ask him
to ask himself, what demand political honour could
have made with which I failed to comply ?

In the ensuing debate on the Address (February 4,
1845), Lord John Russell, in terms of courtesy and
kindness which I had little deserved from him, called
for an explanation of the cause of my retirement. In
a statement which I corrected for ' Hansard's Debates,'
I replied that it had reference to the intentions of the
Government with respect to Maynooth ; that those
intentions pointed to a measure " at variance with the
system which I had maintained," " in a form the most
detailed and deliberate," " in a published treatise :"
that although I had never set forth any theory of
political affairs as " under all circumstances inflexible
and immutable," yet I thought those who had borne
such solemn testimony to a particular view of a great

constitutional question, " ought not to be parties responsible for proposals which involved a material departure from it." And the purpose of my retirement was to " place myself, so far as in me lay, in a position to form not only an honest, but likewise an independent and an unsuspected judgment," on the plan likely to be submitted by the Government. I also spoke as follows, in more forms than one :

" I wish again and most distinctly to state, that I am not prepared to take part in any religious warfare against that measure, such as I believe it may be; or to draw a distinction between the Roman Catholics and other denominations of Christians, with reference to the religious opinions which each of them respectively may hold."

Now I respectfully submit that by this act my freedom was established ; and that it has never since, during a period of nearly five-and-twenty years, been compromised.

Some may say that it is perfectly consistent to have endowed Maynooth anew, and yet to uphold on principle, as a part of the Constitution, the Established Church of Ireland. It may be consistent, for them ; it was not consistent, as I have distinctly shown, for me. The moment that I admitted the validity of a claim by the Church of Rome for the gift, by the free act of the Imperial Parliament, of new funds for the education of its clergy, the true basis of the Established Church of Ireland for me was cut away. The one had always been treated by me as exclusive of the other. It is not now the question whether this way of looking at the question was a correct one. There are great authorities against it ; while it seems at the same time to have some considerable hold on what may be termed the moral sense of portions, perhaps large portions, of the people. The present question is one of fact. It is enough for the present purpose, that such was my view. From that day forward, I have never to my knowledge said one word, in public or in private, which could pledge me on principle to the maintenance of the Irish Church. Nay, in a speech, delivered on the second reading of the Maynooth College Bill, I took occasion distinctly to convey, that the application of religious considerations to ecclesiastical questions in Ireland would be entirely altered by the passing of the measure :—

"The boon to which I for one have thus agreed, is a very great boon. I think it important, most of all important with regard to the principles it involves. I am very far, indeed, from saying that it virtually decides upon the payment of the Roman Catholic priests of Ireland by the State : but I do not deny that it disposes of the religious objections to that measure. I mean that we, who assent to this Bill, shall in my judgment no longer be in a condition to plead religious objections to such a project." [*]

True, I did not say that I was thenceforward prepared at any moment to vote for the removal of the Established Church in Ireland. And this for the best of all reasons : it would not have been true. It is one thing to lift the anchor ; it is another to spread the sails. It may be a duty to be in readiness for departure, when departure itself would be an offence against public prudence and public principle. But I do not go so far even as this. On the contrary, I was willing and desirous [†] that it should be permitted to continue. If its ground in logic was gone, yet it might have, in fact, like much besides, its day of

* 'Speech on the Second Reading of the Maynooth College Bill,' 1845, p. 44.                    † *Ibid.,* p. 33.

grace. I do not now say that I leapt at once to the
conclusion that the Established Church of Ireland
must at any definite period "cease to exist as an
Establishment." She had my sincere good will; I
was not sorry, I was glad, that while Ireland seemed
content to have it so, a longer time should be granted
her to unfold her religious energies through the
medium of an active and pious clergy, which until
this our day she had never possessed. My mind
recoiled then, as it recoils now, from the idea of
worrying the Irish Church to death. I desired that
it should remain even as it was, until the way should
be opened, and the means at hand, for bringing about
some better state of things.

Moreover, it was a duty, from my point of view,
completely to exhaust every chance on behalf of the
Irish Church. I have not been disposed, at any
time of life, gratuitously to undertake agitation of the
most difficult, and at times apparently the most hopeless questions. At the period of the Appropriation
Clause, I represented to myself, and I believe to
others, that the true power of the Church as a religious
engine had never up to that period been fairly tried.
In name a religious institution, her influences, her
benefices, her sees, were commonly employed for purposes, which we must condemn as secular, even if
they had not been utterly *anti-national*. Only within
a few, a very few years, had her clergy even
begun to bestir themselves; and they had forthwith
found that, from the unsettled state of the law of
tithe, they were in the midst of an agitation, both
menacing to public order, and even perilous to
life. I was desirous to see what, after person and
property should have been rendered secure, and a

peaceful atmosphere restored, a generation of pious and zealous men could accomplish in their actual position. I am still of the opinion that thirty-five years ago the religion of the Irish Church had not— to her and to our shame be it spoken—had fair play. From the days of Elizabeth downwards, with the rarest exceptions, the worldly element had entirely outweighed the religious one (whatever the intention may have been) in the actual working of the ecclesiastical institutions of Ireland. Mr. Burke has immortalised the burning shame and the hideous scandals of those penal laws which, perhaps for the first time in the history of Christendom if not of man, aimed at persecuting men out of one religion, but not at persecuting them into another. I will not be so rash as to enter on the field—

"Per quem magnus equos Auruncæ flexit alumnus."

But the time of awakening had come. The Irish Church had grown conscious that she had a Gospel to declare. Even with my present opinions I might feel a scruple as to the measures now proposed, but for the resistless and accumulated proof of impotence afforded by the experience of my life-time, and due, I believe, to a radically false position. For the Irish Church has, since the tithe war of 1830-2 came to an end, had not only fair play—that is such fair play as in Ireland the Establishment allows to the Church— but fair play and something more. She has enjoyed an opportunity, extending over a generation of men, with circumstances of favour such as can hardly be expected to recur. What has been her case? She has had ample endowments; perfect security; an

D

almost unbroken freedom from the internal controversies which have chastened (though, in chastening,
I believe improved) the Church of England. The
knowledge of the Irish language has been extensively
attained by her clergy.* She has had all the moral
support that could be given her by the people of this
country; for it was the people, and not a mere party,
who, in 1835-8, repudiated and repelled the Appropriation Clause. Her rival, the Church of Rome,
has seen its people borne down to the ground by
famine; and then thinned from year to year, in hun-
dreds of thousands, by the resistless force of emigration. And, last and most of all, in the midst of that
awful visitation of 1847-8, her Protestant Clergy
came to the Roman Catholic people clad in the garb
of angels of light; for, besides their own bounty
(most liberal, I believe, in proportion to their means),
they became the grand almoners of the British nation.
When, after all this, we arrive at a new census of
religion in 1861, we find that only the faintest impression has been made upon the relative numbers
of the two bodies; an impression much slighter, I
apprehend, than would have been due to the comparative immunity of the Established Church from
the drain of emigration; and, if so, representing in
reality, not a gain, but a virtual loss of some part
of the narrow ground which before was occupied by
the favoured religion of the State.

　　Like others, I have watched with interest the
results of those missionary operations in the West
of Ireland which have, perhaps, been construed as of
a greater ulterior significance than really belongs to

---

* See ' Life of Archbishop Whately.'

them. They were, I understand, due not so much to
the Established Church, as to religious bodies in this
country, which expend large funds in Ireland for the
purpose of making converts: an operation in which
the Presbyterians and Protestant Dissenters lend their
aid. Let them not be undervalued. But I, for one,
recollect that this is not the first time when local
and occasional inroads have been successfully effected
by Protestants upon the serried phalanx of the
Roman Church in Ireland, and have been mistaken
for signs of permanent or a general conquest. More
than forty years ago, Bishop Blomfield — no mean
authority—prophesied or announced, in the House of
Lords, that a second Reformation had then begun.
And there had indeed taken place in Ireland at that
time one, if not more than one, instance of conver-
sions on a large scale to the Established Church,
such as was well calculated to excite sanguine antici-
pations, though they were dispelled by subsequent
experience. I think we ought now to perceive that
the annexation of the warrant of civil authority to
the religious embassy of the Irish Church, discredits
in lieu of recommending it in the view of the Irish
people. I do not mean that we are to put down the
Establishment for the sake of a more effective propa-
gandism. We must not for a moment forget that
civil justice, an adaptation of the state of things in
Ireland to the essential principles of political right, is
that one broad and more than sufficient justification
of the measure, in which all its advocates agree. But,
over and above this, they may also agree in reflecting
with satisfaction that the time is about to come when
in Ireland, in lieu of a system which insults the re-

ligion of the majority and makes that of the minority powerless, creeds will compete upon the level, and will thrive according to their merits. Nor will they be offended with one another when, in the anticipation of such a state of things, each man who has faith in freedom, faith in justice, faith in truth, anticipates a harvest of benefit for his own.

The emancipation thus effected from the net in which I had been bound was soon after tested. In 1846, it was suggested to me that I should oppose a member of the newly-formed Government of Lord John Russell. In my reply, declining the proposal, I wrote thus: " As to the Irish Church, I am not able to go to war with them on the ground that they will not pledge themselves to the maintenance of the existing appropriation of Church property in Ireland." This, however, was a private proceeding. But, early in 1847, Mr. Estcourt announced his resignation of the seat he had held, amidst universal respect, for the University of Oxford. The partiality of friends proposed me as a candidate. The representation of that University was, I think, stated by Mr. Canning to be to him the most coveted prize of political life. I am not ashamed to own that I desired it with an almost passionate fondness. For besides all the associations it maintained and revived, it was in those days an honour not only given without solicitation, but, when once given, not withdrawn.* The contest was conducted with much activity, and some heat. I was, naturally enough, challenged as to my opinions on the Established Church of Ireland. My

* The case of Sir R. Peel, in 1829, I do not consider an exception to this remark, as he gave back the charge into the hands of the electors.

friend Mr. Coleridge, then young, but already distinguished, was one of my most active and able
supporters.  He has borne spontaneous testimony,
within the last few weeks, to the manner in which
the challenge was met :—

"Gentlemen, I must be permitted—because an attack has
been made upon Mr. Gladstone, and it has been suggested
that his conversion to his present principles is recent—to
mention what is within my own knowledge and experience
with regard to him.  In 1847, when I was just leaving
Oxford, I had the great honour of being secretary to his first
election committee for that university, and I well recollect
how, upon that occasion, some older and more moderate
supporters were extremely anxious to draw from him some
pledge that he should stand by the Irish Church.  He distinctly refused to pledge himself to anything of the kind." *

The next Parliamentary occasion, after the Maynooth Grant, which brought prominently into view
the ecclesiastical arrangements of Ireland, was that
of the Ecclesiastical Titles Bill in 1851.  I felt bound,
as one of a very small minority, but in cordial agree-
ment with the chief surviving associates of Sir Robert
Peel, to offer all the opposition in my power, not
only to the clauses by which the party then called
Protectionist, and now Tory, Conservative, or Con-
stitutionalist, endeavoured to sharpen the sting of the
measure, but to the substance of the measure itself.  I
may be permitted to observe, that for the representa-
tive of the University of Oxford thus to set himself
against the great bulk of the Liberal as well as the
Conservative party, whatever else it may have been,
was not a servile or a self-seeking course.  But this

* Mr. Coleridge's speech at Exeter, August, 1868.  From the 'Man
chester Examiner' of August 22.

is irrelevant. It is more to the present purpose to observe that, in resisting this measure, I did not attempt to mitigate the offence by any profession of adhesion in principle to the maintenance of the Established Church of Ireland; but I spoke as follows :—

"We cannot change the profound and resistless tendencies of the age towards religious liberty. It is our business to guide and control their application. Do this you may. But to endeavour to turn them backwards is the sport of children, done by the hands of men; and every effort you may make in that direction will recoil upon you in disaster and disgrace." *

The years flowed on. From 1846 forwards, the controversy of Free Trade was, as a rule, the commanding and absorbing controversy, the pole of political affairs. But from time to time motions were made in relation to the Established Church of Ireland. That question remained as one asleep, but whose sleep is haunted with uneasy dreams. These motions were, as far as I remember them, uniformly of a narrow and partial character. They aimed at what is called getting in the thin end of the wedge. All honour, however, to each one of those who made them. The mover of any such proposal was *vox clamantis in deserto*. The people of England had, in 1835-8, settled the matter for the time. The reproaches now made against the older leaders and the body of the Liberal party for not having seriously entered the struggle, appear to me to be not only unjust but even preposterous. The Legislature had other great subjects to deal with, besides the Irish Church. Four years of deadly conflict on such a

* 'Corrected Speech on the Ecclesiastical Titles Bill,' 1851, p. 28.

matter might well be followed by five times four of repose. But in the mean time individuals, by their partial and occasional efforts, bore witness to a principle broader than any which they formally announced. That principle—the application of a true religious equality to Ireland—was biding its time.

No one, in my opinion, was bound to assert, by speech or vote, any decisive opinion upon so great and formidable a question until he should think, upon a careful survey of the ground and the time, of the assisting and opposing forces, that the season for action had come. The motions actually made were commonly motions for inquiry, or motions aimed generally at a change. I did not enter into the debates. When I voted, I voted against them; and against such motions, if they were made, I should vote again.

I now arrive at the Government of 1859-65. He who has slept long is likely soon to wake. After the Free Trade struggles of 1860 and 1861 were over, so it was, I thought, with the question of the Irish Church. There was a lull in political affairs. They hung, in a great degree, upon a single life—the remarkable life of Lord Palmerston. It was surely right to think a little of the future. The calm was certain to be succeeded by a breeze, if not a gale. It was too plain to me that the inner disposition of Ireland, relatively to this country, was not improving; and that, in the course of years, more or fewer, the question of the Irish Church was certain to revive, and, if it should revive, probably to be carried to a final issue. My first thought, under these circumstances, was about my constituents. Anxiously occupied in other matters, I did not give my nights and days to the question of the Irish Church. Yet the question continually flitted, as it were, before me; and I felt that, before that question arose in a practical shape, my relation to the University should be considered, and its Convocation distinctly apprised that at the proper time it would be my duty to support very extensive changes in the Irish Church. My valued friend, Sir R. Palmer, has done me the favour, of his own motion, to state in public that I then apprised him of my state of mind :—

"There had been people who had said, ' You would never have heard anything about the Irish Church question from Mr. Gladstone if the Tories had not been in power, and he had not wanted to get their place.' (Hear, hear.) To his certain knowledge that was not true. He could mention what had taken place between Mr. Gladstone and himself, and he did so the rather because it did justice to him, and would show them that his own mind had been particularly addressed to that subject, to which he had paid some degree of attention some years before the present time. In the year 1863, at a time when no one was bringing forward this question, or seemed very likely to do so, Mr. Gladstone had told him privately that he had made up his mind on the subject, and that he should not be able to keep himself from giving public expression to his feelings. How far or near that might be practicable, he could not foresee; but, under the circumstances, he wanted his friends connected with the University of Oxford to consider whether or not they would desire for that reason a change in the representation of the University." *

* Sir R. Palmer's speech at Richmond, August, 1868. From the 'Manchester Examiner' of August 24.

Partly because I felt that this question might come to the front, and partly because I saw a manifest determination in a portion of the Academical constituency to press my friends with incessant contests, of which I was unwilling to be the hero, I was not indisposed to retire without compulsion from the seat, if it could have been done without obvious detriment to the principles on which I had been returned. This was judged to be uncertain. Consequently, I remained. But in 1865, on the motion of Mr. Dillwyn, I made a speech, in which I declared that present action was impossible, that at any period immense difficulties would have to be encountered, but that this was " the question of the future." I stated strongly, though summarily, some of the arguments against the Church as it stood. I entirely abstained from advising or glancing at the subject of mere reform, and I did not use one word from which it could be inferred that I desired it to continue in its place as the National or Established Church of the country.

My speech was immediately denounced by Mr. (now Chief Justice) Whiteside, as one intended to be fatal to the Established Church of Ireland when an opportunity should arise ;* and I am told that my opponents in the University circulated my speech among their portion of the constituency (as I think they were quite justified in doing) to my prejudice. My friends, however, stood by me, and resolved to

* ' Hansard,' vol. clxxviii. p. 444.—" But I do complain of a Minister who, himself the author of a book in defence of Church and State, when one branch of the Christian Church is attacked and in danger, delivers a speech, every word of which is hostile to its existence when the right time comes for attacking it."

contend for the seat. An application was made to me by a distinguished scholar, divine, and teacher, the Warden of Trinity College, Glenalmond, to give certain explanations for the appeasing of doubts. I did so in the following letter :—

"11, Carlton House Terrace, S.W., June 8, 1865.

"DEAR DR. HANNAH,

"It would be very difficult for me to subscribe to *any* interpretation of my speech on the Irish Church like that of your correspondent, which contains so many conditions and bases of a plan for dealing with a question apparently remote, and at the same time full of difficulties on every side. My reasons are, I think, plain. First, because the question is remote, and apparently out of all bearing on the practical politics of the day, I think it would be for me worse than superfluous to determine upon any scheme or basis of a scheme with respect to it. Secondly, because it is difficult, even if I anticipated any likelihood of being called upon to deal with it, I should think it right to make no decision beforehand on the mode of dealing with the difficulties. But the first reason is that which chiefly weighs. As far as I know, my speech signifies pretty clearly the broad distinction which I take between the abstract and the practical views of the subject. And I think I have stated strongly my sense of the responsibility attaching to the opening of such a question, except in a state of things which gave promise of satisfactorily closing it. For this reason it is that I have been so silent about the matter, and may probably be so again ; but I could not as a Minister, and as member for Oxford, allow it to be debated an indefinite number of times and remain silent. One thing, however, I may add, because I think it a clear landmark. In any measure dealing with the Irish Church, I think (though I scarcely *expect* ever to. be called on to share in such a measure) the Act of Union must be recognised and must have important consequences, especially with reference to the position of the hierarchy.

"I am much obliged to you for writing, and I hope you

will see and approve my reasons for not wishing to carry my *own mind* further into a question lying at a distance I cannot measure.

> " Yours sincerely,
>
> (Signed) " W. E. GLADSTONE.

"Rev. the WARDEN, Trin. Coll., Perth."

The letter has been the object of much criticism upon these three grounds. First, it contained a statement that the Act of Union ought to entail important consequences in the formation of any measure relating to the Irish Church. Secondly, that the question was hardly within the domain of practical politics. Thirdly, that I felt very uncertain whether it would be dealt with in my time. The explanation of the first is as follows :—In contemplating the subject of the Irish Church, I did not see how to give full effect to the principle of religious equality without touching the composition of the House of Lords. In this strait, my personal opinion was that it would be best to retain (though in an altered form) the Episcopal element from Ireland in the House of Lords, lest its withdrawal should lead to other changes, of a kind to weaken the constitution of that important branch of the legislature ; and thus far I was disposed to abridge the application of religious equality to Ireland. I had not yet examined the question so closely as to perceive that this mode of proceeding was wholly impracticable, and that the inconvenience of removing the Irish Bishops must be faced. And for my part I have not been so happy, at any time of my life, as to be able sufficiently to adjust the proper conditions of handling any difficult

question, until the question itself was at the door.
This retention of the Bishops in the House of Peers
was the important consequence that I thought the
Act of Union would draw.

Among those errors of the day which may be
called singular as vulgar errors, is that which sup-
poses the fifth Article of the Act of Union with Ireland to refer to the endowments of the Church. Its
terms touch exclusively her " doctrine, worship,
discipline, and government." There is no violation of
this section of the Act of Union in withdrawing her
endowments, were she stripped of every shilling. But
it may be said that her " government," as distinguished
from her discipline, perhaps involves the position of
her exclusive relation to the State. So I thought;
and accordingly thus I wrote to Dr. Hannah.

The second proposition of the letter was not only
in harmony with my speech, it was simply the con-
densation of the speech into a brief form of words.
For, agreeing with Mr. Dillwyn as to the merits of
the case, I held, as I have ever held, that it is not
the duty of a Minister to be forward in inscribing on
the Journals of Parliament his own abstract views;
or to disturb the existence of a great institution like
the Church of Ireland, until he conceives the time to
be come when he can probably give effect to his
opinions. Because the question was not within the
range of practical politics, agreeing with his sentiment, I voted against his motion.

But, forsooth, it is a matter of wonder that I should
have felt doubtful whether the Irish Church would
be dealt with in my time. Now, I do not complain
of this. It is an example of what is continually hap-

pening in human affairs, of the mythical handling of
facts, of the reflection of the ideas, feelings, and circumstances of one period upon the events of another, and
thus dressing the past in the garb of the present.    I
abide by this, and by every word of the letter.    The
question of the Irish Church was in my view, in the
year 1865, what, be it remembered, the question of
Parliamentary Reform seemed to be in the first moiety -
of the year 1830—namely, a remote question.    Had
any man said to me, " How soon will it come on ? "
I should have replied, " Heaven knows; perhaps it
will be five years, perhaps it will be ten."    My duty
was to let my constituents know the state of my
mind on a matter so important, because the wind was
gradually veering to that quarter, even though I
might not believe, and did not believe it to be the
most probable event, that it would reach the point
for action during the life of the Parliament just then
about to be elected.    But then I referred to my own
political lifetime.    On that subject I will only say
that a man who, in 1865, completed his thirty-third
year of a laborious career ; who had already followed
to the grave the remains of almost all the friends
abreast of whom he had started from the University
in the career of public life ; and who had observed
that, excepting two recent cases, it was hard to find
in our whole history a single man who had been
permitted to reach the fortieth year of a course of
labour similar to his own within the walls of the
House of Commons ; such a man might surely be
excused if he did not venture to reckon for himself
on an exemption from the lot of greater and better
men, and if he formed a less sanguine estimate of the

fraction of space yet remaining to him, than seems to
have been the case with his critics.

The reasons that, in my judgment, prove the time
now to have arrived for dealing decisively with the
question of the Irish Church Establishment, must be
treated elsewhere than in these pages.

So far as Ireland, and the immediate controversy,
and my personal vindication are concerned, I have
done. But there is matter of wider interest, which
connects itself with the subject. The change of conduct, the shifting of the mind of an individual,
shrink into insignificance by the side of the question,
What has been, since 1838, the direction of the public
sentiment, the course of law and administration, the
general march of affairs ?

I have described the erroneous impressions as to
the actual and prospective state of things, under
which was urged the practical application of that
system of thought embodied in my work of 1838.
It may be said my error was a gross or even an
absurd one. On that question I need not enter. But
I will endeavour to bring into view some circumstances relating to the time, which may help to
account for it. And here I feel that I pass beyond
the narrower and more personal scope of these pages,
if I attempt to recall some of the changes that have
taken place during the last thirty or five-and-thirty
years, in matters which bear upon the religious
character and relations of the State.

At that time, Jews, and others not adopting the
Christian name, were excluded from civil office ; and
though Roman Catholics and Nonconformists had
effected an entrance into Parliament, there still re-

mained an oath for the former, and a declaration for
the latter, which, if they did not practically limit
freedom, yet denoted, like the mark of chains on the
limbs of an emancipated slave, that there had been a
time when it did not exist.   The Establishment of
Scotland was still entire, and animated with the
strength principally of the eminent men who afterwards led the Free Church Secession.   The attack on
the Irish Church, pushed in 1835 with earnestness
and vigour by the Liberal party, had speedily proved
to be hopeless.   The State continued to make to other
persuasions certain grants, little more than compas-
sionate, and handed down from other times; but, even
in the case of the classes especially in its charge, such
as soldiers and sailors, or such again as paupers and
criminals, it rarely permitted, and still more rarely
provided for them, the means of religious worship
according to their own religious convictions.   In the
great province of popular education in England,
nothing was granted except to schools of the Church,
or to schools in which, while the Bible was read, no
religion other than that of the Church was taught;
and he would have been deemed something more
than a daring prophet, who should have foretold that
in a few years the utmost ambition of the lay cham-
pions, and of the spiritual heads of the Church,
would be to obtain the maintenance of a denomina-
tional system in popular education, under which all
religions alike should receive the indirect, yet not
unsubstantial, countenance of the State.

But the most important of all the changes which
have taken place within the interval, has been the

change in the condition of the Church of England itself.

Even for those old enough to have an adequate recollection of the facts, it requires no inconsiderable mental effort to travel backwards over the distractions, controversies, perils, and calamities of the last thirty years, to the period immediately before those years; and to realise not only the state of facts, but especially the promises and prospects which it presented. I am well aware that any description of it which may now be attempted will appear to bear more or less the colour of romance; but, without taking it into view, no one can either measure the ground over which we have travelled, or perceive how strong was then the temptation to form an oversanguine estimate of the probable progress of the Church in her warfare with sin and ignorance, and even in persuading seceders of all kinds to re-enter her fold.

That time was a time such as comes, after sickness, to a man in the flower of life, with an unimpaired and buoyant constitution; the time in which, though health is as yet incomplete, the sense and the joy of health are keener, as the fresh and living current first flows in, than are conveyed by its even and undisturbed possession.

The Church of England had been passing through a long period of deep and chronic religious lethargy. For many years, perhaps for some generations, Christendom might have been challenged to show, either then or from any former age, a clergy (with exceptions) so secular and lax, or congregations so cold, irreverent, and indevout. The process of awakening had, indeed, begun many years before ; but a very long time is required to stir up effectually a torpid body, whose dimensions overspread a great country.　Active piety and zeal among the clergy, and yet more among the laity, had been in a great degree confined within the narrow limits of a party, which, however meritorious in its work, presented in the main phenomena of transition, and laid but little hold on the higher intellect and cultivation of the country.　Our churches and our worship bore in general too conclusive testimony to a frozen indifference.　No effort had been made either to overtake the religious destitution of the multitudes at home, or to follow the numerous children of the Church, migrating into distant lands, with any due provision for their spiritual wants.　The richer benefices were very commonly regarded as a suitable provision for such members of the higher families as were least fit to push their way in any profession requiring thought or labour.　The abuses of plurality and non-residence were at a height, which, if not proved by statistical returns, it would now be scarcely possible to believe.　In the greatest public school of the country (and I presume it may be taken as a sample of the rest) the actual teaching of Christianity was all but dead, though happily none of its forms had been surrendered.　It is a retrospect full of gloom ; and with all our Romanising, and all our Rationalising, what man of sense would wish to go back upon those dreary times :

"Domos Ditis vacuas, et inania regna "?*

* Æn. vi.

E

But between 1831 and 1840, the transformation, which had previously begun, made a progress altogether marvellous. Much was due, without doubt, to the earnest labour of individuals. Such men as Bishop Blomfield on the Bench, and Dr. Hook in the parish (and I name them only as illustrious examples), who had long been toiling with a patient but a dauntless energy, began as it were to get the upper hand. But causes of deep and general operation were also widely at work. As the French Revolution had done much to renovate Christian belief on the Continent, so the Church of England was less violently, but pretty sharply, roused by the political events which arrived in a rattling succession. In 1828, the repeal of the Test Act. In 1829, the emancipation of the Roman Catholics. In 1831-2, the agony and triumph of Reform. In 1833, the Church Temporalities Act for Ireland. There was now a general uprising of religious energy in the Church throughout the land. It saved the Church. Her condition before 1830 could not possibly have borne the scrutinising eye, which for thirty years past has been turned upon our institutions. Her rank corruptions must have called down the avenging arm. But it was arrested just in time.

It would be difficult to give a just and full idea of the beneficial changes which were either accomplished or begun during this notable decade of years. They embraced alike formal, official movements, of a nature to strike the general eye, and those local improvements in detail, which singly are known only in each neighbourhood, but which unitedly transform the face of a country. Laws were passed to repress

gross abuses, and the altering spirit of the clergy
seconded and even outstripped the laws. The outward face of divine worship began to be renovated,
and the shameful condition of the sacred fabrics was
rapidly amended, with such a tide of public approval
as overflowed all the barriers of party and of sect,
and speedily found its manifestations even in the
seceding communions. There is no reason to doubt
that at that time at least, and before such changes
had become too decidedly the fashion, the outward
embellishment of churches, and the greater decency
and order of services, answered to, and sprang from,
a call within, and proved a less unworthy conception
of the sublime idea of Christian worship. The missionary arm of the Church began to exhibit a vigour
wholly unknown to former years. Noble efforts
were made, under the auspices of the chief bishops
of the Church, to provide for the unsatisfied spiritual
wants of the metropolis. The great scheme of the
Colonial Episcopate was founded ; and, in its outset, led
to such a development of apostolic zeal and self-denial
as could not but assist, by a powerful reaction, the
domestic progress. The tone of public schools (on one
of which Arnold was now spending his noble energies)
and of universities, was steadily yet rapidly raised.
The greatest change of all was within the body of
the clergy.* A devoted piety and an unworldly life,
which had been the rare exceptions, became visibly
from year to year more and more the rule. The

* It was, I think, about the year 1835, that I first met the Rev. Sydney
Smith, at the house of Mr. Hallam. In conversation after dinner he said to
me, with the double charm of humour and of good-humour, " The improve-
ment of the clergy in my time has been astonishing. Whenever you meet
a clergyman of my age, you may be quite sure that he is a bad clergyman."

spectacle, as a whole, was like what we are told of a
Russian spring : when, after long months of rigid
cold, almost in a day the snow dissolves, the ice
breaks up and is borne away, and the whole earth is
covered with a rush of verdure.  These were bright
and happy days for the Church of England.  She
seemed, or seemed to seem, as a Church recalling the
descriptions of Holy Writ; to be "beautiful as the
sun which goeth forth in his might," * " and terrible
as an army with banners." †

Of this great renovating movement, a large part
centred in Oxford.  At the time, indeed, when I
resided there, from 1828 to 1831, no sign of it had
yet appeared.  A steady, clear, but dry Anglican
orthodoxy bore sway, and frowned, this way or that,
on the first indication of any tendency to diverge
from the beaten path.  Dr. Pusey was, at that time,
revered, indeed, for his piety and charity, no less than
admired for his learning and talents, but suspected
(I believe) of sympathy with the German theology,
in which he was known to be profoundly versed.
Dr. Newman was thought to have about him the
flavour of what, he has now told the world, were
the opinions he had derived in youth from the works
of Thomas Scott.  Mr. Keble, the "sweet singer of
Israel," and a true saint, if this generation has seen
one, did not reside in Oxford.‡  The chief Chair of
Theology had been occupied by Bishop Lloyd, the
old tutor and the attached and intimate friend of

---

* Judges, v. 31.          † Canticles, vi. 4.
‡ Since these lines were written I have learned, upon authority which
cannot be questioned, that Mr. Keble acknowledged the justice of disestab-
lishing the Irish Church.

Peel : a man of powerful talents, and of a character
both winning and decided, who, had his life been
spared, might have acted powerfully for good on the
fortunes of the Church of England, by guiding the
energetic influences which his teaching had done
much to form. But he had been hurried away in 1829
by an early death : and Dr. Whately, who was also,
in his own way, a known power in the University,
was in 1830 induced to accept the Archbishopric
of Dublin. There was nothing at that time in the
theology, or in the religious life, of the University
to indicate what was to come. But when, shortly
afterwards, the great heart of England began to beat
with the quickened pulsations of a more energetic
religious life, it was in Oxford that the stroke was
most distinct and loud. An extraordinary change
appeared to pass upon the spirit of the place. I
believe it would be a moderate estimate to say that
much beyond one half of the very flower of its youth
chose the profession of Holy Orders, while an impression scarcely less deep seemed to be stamped
upon a large portion of its lay pupils. I doubt
whether at any period of its existence, either since
the Reformation, or perhaps before it, the Church of
England had reaped from either University, in so
short a time, so rich a harvest. At Cambridge a
similar lifting up of heart and mind seems to have
been going on ; and numbers of persons of my own
generation, who at their public schools had been
careless and thoughtless like the rest, appeared in
their early manhood as soldiers of Christ, and ministers to the wants of His people, worthy, I believe,
as far as man can be worthy, through their zeal,
devotion, powers of mind, and attainments, of their

high vocation. It was not then foreseen what storms were about to rise. Not only in Oxford, but in England, during the years to which I refer, party spirit within the Church was reduced to a low ebb. Indiscretions there might be, but authority did not take alarm : it smiled rather, on the contrary, on what was thought to be in the main a recurrence both to first principles and to forgotten obligations. Purity, unity, and energy seemed, as three fair sisters hand in hand, to advance together. Such a state of things was eminently suited to act on impressible and sanguine minds. I, for one, formed a completely false estimate of what was about to happen ; and believed that the Church of England, through the medium of a regenerated clergy and an intelligent and attached laity, would not only hold her ground, but would even in great part probably revive the love and the allegiance both of the masses who were wholly falling away from religious observances, and of those large and powerful nonconforming bodies, the existence of which was supposed to have no other cause than the neglect of its duties by the National Church, which had long left the people as sheep without a shepherd.

And surely it would have required either a deeply saturnine or a marvellously prophetic mind to foretell that, in ten or twelve more years, that powerful and distinguished generation of clergy would be broken up : that at least a moiety of the most gifted sons, whom Oxford had reared for the service of the Church of England, would be hurling at her head the hottest bolts of the Vatican : that, with their deviation on the one side, there would arise a not less convulsive rationalistic movement on the other ; and

that the natural consequences would be developed in
endless contention and estrangement, and in sus-
picions worse than either, because even less accessible,
and even more intractable. Since that time, the
Church of England may be said to have bled at
every pore; and at this hour it seems occasionally
to quiver to its very base. And yet, all the while,
the religious life throbs more and more powerfully
within her. Shorn of what may be called the
romance and poetry of her revival, she abates nothing
of her toil; and in the midst of every sort of partial
indiscretion and extravagance, her great office in the
care of souls is, from year to year, less and less
imperfectly discharged. But the idea of asserting
on her part those exclusive claims, which become
positively unjust in a divided country governed on
popular principles, has been abandoned by all parties
in the State.

There was an error not less serious in my estimate
of English Nonconformity. I remember the astonish-
ment with which at some period,—I think in 1851-2,
—after ascertaining the vast addition which had
been made to the number of churches in the country,
I discovered that the multiplication of chapels, among
those not belonging to the Church of England, had
been more rapid still. But besides the immense
extension of its material and pastoral organisation,
English Nonconformity (in general) appears now to
have founded itself on a principle of its own, which
forbids the alliance of the civil power with religion
in any particular form or forms. I do not embrace
that principle. But I must observe, in passing, that
it is not less unjust than it is common to stigmatise
those who hold it as "political Dissenters,"—a phrase

implying that they do not dissent on religious grounds. But if they, because they object to the union of Church and State, are political Dissenters, it follows that all who uphold it are political Churchmen.

The entire miscalculation which I have now endeavoured to describe of the religious state and prospects of the country, was combined with a view of the relative position of governors and governed, since greatly modified; and the two lay at the root of my error. These two causes led me into the excess of recommending the continued maintenance of a theory which was impracticable, and which, if it could have been enforced, would have been, under the circumstances of the country, less than just. For I never held that a National Church should be permanently maintained except for the nation,—I mean either for the whole of it or, at least, for the greater part, with some kind of real concurrence or general acquiescence from the remainder.

Against the proposals of my book, Lord Macaulay had set up a theory of his own.*

"That we may give Mr. Gladstone his revenge, we will state concisely our own views respecting the alliance of Church and State. . . . .

"We consider the primary end of Government as a purely temporal end, the protection of the persons and property of men.

"We think that Government, like every other contrivance of human wisdom, from the highest to the lowest, is likely to answer its main end best, when it is constructed with a single view to that end. . . . .

"Government is not an institution for the propagation of religion, any more than St. George's Hospital is an institution for the propagation of religion. And the most absurd and

* 'Ed. Rev.', April, 1839, p. 273-6.

pernicious consequences would follow if Government should
pursue as its primary end, that which can never be more
than its secondary end: though intrinsically more important
than its primary end. But a Government which considers
the religious instruction of the people as a secondary end,
and follows out that principle faithfully, will we think be
likely to do much good and little harm."

These sentences, I think, give a fair view of Lord
Macaulay's philosophy of Church Establishments. It
has all the clearness and precision that might be
expected from him. But I own myself unable to
accept it as it stands. I presume to think that perhaps Lord Macaulay, like myself, made, from a limited
induction, a hasty generalisation. The difference
was, that his theory was right for the practical purpose of the time, while mine was wrong. Considered,
however, in the abstract, that theory appears to me
to claim kindred with the ethical code of another
writer, not less upright, and not less limpid, so to
speak, than Lord Macaulay himself, I mean Dr. Paley.
And the upshot of it may be comprised in three words:
Government is police. All other functions, except
those of police proper, are the accidents of its existence. As if a man should say to his friend when in
the country, "I am going up to town; can I take
anything for you?" So the State, while busy about
protecting life and property, will allow its officer of
police to perform any useful office for the community,
to instruct a wayfarer as to his road, or tell the passer
by what o'clock it is, provided it does not interfere
with his watching the pickpocket, or laying the
strong hand upon the assassin. I doubt if it is possible to cut out, as it were, with a pair of scissors,

patterns of policy, which shall solve for all time and place the great historic problem of the relation of the civil power to religion.

It seems to me that in every function of life, and in every combination with his fellow-creatures, for whatever purpose, the duties of man are limited only by his powers. It is easy to separate, in the case of a Gas Company or a Chess Club, the primary end for which it exists, from everything extraneous to that end. It is not so easy in the case of the State or of the family. If the primary end of the State is to protect life and property, so the primary end of the family is to propagate the race. But around these ends there cluster, in both cases, a group of moral purposes, variable indeed with varying circumstances, but yet inhering in the relation, and not external or merely incidental to it. The action of man in the State is moral, as truly as it is in the individual sphere; although it be limited by the fact that, as he is combined with others whose views and wills may differ from his own, the sphere of the common operations must be limited, first, to the things in which all are agreed; secondly, to the things in which, though they may not be agreed, yet equity points out, and the public sense acknowledges, that the whole should be bound by the sense of the majority.

I can hardly believe that even those, including as they do so many men both upright and able, who now contend on principle for the separation of the Church from the State, are so determined to exalt their theorem to the place of an universal truth, that they ask us to condemn the whole of that process, by

which, as the Gospel spread itself through the civi-
lised world, Christianity became incorporated with the
action of civil authority, and with the framework of
public law.  In the course of human history, indeed,
we perceive little of unmixed evil, and far less of
universal good.  It is not difficult to discern that (in
the language of Bishop Heber) as the world became
Christian, Christianity became worldly; that the
average tone of a system, which embraces in its
wide-spreading arms the entire community, is almost
of necessity lower than that of a society which, if
large, is still private, and into which no man enters
except by his own deliberate choice, very possibly even
at the cost of much personal and temporal detriment.
But Christ died for the race : and those who notice
the limited progress of conversion in the world until
alliance with the civil authority gave to His religion
a wider access to the attention of mankind, may be
inclined to doubt whether, without that alliance, its
immeasurable and inestimable social results would
ever have been attained.  Allowing for all that may
be justly urged against the danger of mixing secular
motives with religious administration, and above all
against the intrusion of force into the domain of
thought ; I for one cannot desire that Constantine in
the government of the empire, that Justinian in the
formation of its code of laws, or that Charlemagne in
refounding society, or that Elizabeth in the crisis of
the English Reformation, should have acted on the
principle that the State and the Church in themselves
are separate or alien powers, incapable of coalition.

But there are two causes, the combined operation
of which, upon reaching a certain point of develop-

ment, relaxes or dissolves their union by a process
as normal (if it be less beneficial) as that by which
the union was originally brought about. One of
these is the establishment of the principle of popular
self-government as the basis of political constitutions.
The other is the disintegration of Christendom from
one into many communions. As long as the Church
at large, or the Church within the limits of the nation,
is substantially one, I do not see why the religious
care of the subject, through a body properly consti-
tuted for the purpose, should cease to be a function
of the State, with the whole action and life of which
it has, throughout Europe, been so long and so closely
associated. As long as the State holds, by descent,
by the intellectual superiority of the governing
classes, and by the good will of the people, a position
of original and underived authority, there is no abso-
lute impropriety, but the reverse, in its commending
to the nation the greatest of all boons. But when,
either by some Revolution of institutions from their
summit to their base, or by a silent and surer process,
analogous to that which incessantly removes and
replaces the constituent parts of the human body,
the State has come to be the organ of the deliberate
and ascertained will of the community, expressed
through legal channels—then the inculcation of a
religion can no longer rest, in full or permanent
force, upon its authority. When, in addition to this,
the community itself is split and severed into opinions
and communions, which, whatever their concurrence
in the basis of Christian belief, are hostile in regard
to the point at issue, so that what was meant for the
nation dwindles into the private estate as it were of

a comparative handful—the attempt to maintain an Established Church becomes an error fatal to the peace, dangerous perhaps even to the life, of civil society. Such a Church then becomes (to use a figure I think of John Foster's), no longer the temple, but the mere cemetery, of a great idea. Such a policy is then not simply an attempt to treat what is superannuated and imbecile as if it were full of life and vigour, but to thwart the regular and normal action of the ruling social forces, to force them from their proper channels, and to turn them by artificial contrivance, as Apollo turned the rivers of Troas from their beds, to a purpose of our own. This is to set caprice against nature; and the end must be that, with more or less of delay, more or less of struggle or convulsion, nature will get the better of caprice.

But does it follow from all this, that the tone of moral action in the State should be lowered? Such a fear is what perplexes serious and sober men, who are laudably unwilling to surrender, in a world where falsehood has so wide a range, any portion of this vantage-ground of truth and right. I, who may have helped to mislead them by an over-hasty generalisation, would now submit what seems to me calculated to re-assure the mind. I make an appeal to the history of the last thirty years. During those years, what may be called the dogmatic allegiance of the State to religion has been greatly relaxed; but its consciousness of moral duty has been not less notably quickened and enhanced. I do not say this in depreciation of Christian dogma. But we are still a Christian people. Christianity has wrought itself into the public life of fifteen hundred years. Precious truths, and laws of relative right and the brotherhood of man, such as the wisdom of heathenism scarcely dreamed of and could never firmly grasp, the Gospel has made to be part of our common inheritance, common as the sunlight that warms us, and as the air we breathe. Sharp though our divisions in belief may be, they have not cut so deep as to prevent, or as perceptibly to impair, the recognition of these great guides and fences of moral action. It is far better for us to trust to the operation of these our common principles and feelings, and to serve our Maker together in that wherein we are at one, rather than in aiming at a standard theoretically higher, to set out with a breach of the great commandment, which forms the ground-work of all relative duties, and to refuse to do as we would be done by.

It is, then, by a practical rather than a theoretic test that our Establishments of religion should be tried. In applying this practical test, we must be careful to do it with those allowances, which are as necessary for the reasoner in moral subjects, as it is for the reasoner in mechanics to allow for friction or for the resistance of the air. An Establishment that does its work in much, and has the hope and likeli-hood of doing it in more : an Establishment that has a broad and living way open to it, into the hearts of the people : an Establishment that can commend the services of the present by the recollections and tra-ditions of a far-reaching past : an Establishment able to appeal to the active zeal of the greater portion of the people, and to the respect or scruples of almost the whole, whose children dwell chiefly on her actual living work and service, and whose adversaries, if she

has them, are in the main content to believe that
there will be a future for them and their opinions:
such an Establishment should surely be maintained.
But an Establishment that neither does, nor has her
hope of doing, work, except for a few, and those few
the portion of the community whose claim to public
aid is the smallest of all : an Establishment severed
from the mass of the people by an impassable gulph,
and by a wall of brass : an Establishment whose good
offices, could she offer them, would be intercepted by
a long unbroken chain of painful and shameful recollections : an Establishment leaning for support upon
the extraneous aid of a State, which becomes dis-
credited with the people by the very act of lending
it : such an Establishment will do well for its own
sake, and for the sake of its creed, to divest itself, as
soon as may be, of gauds and trappings, and to com-
mence a new career, in which, renouncing at once the
credit and the discredit of the civil sanction, it shall
seek its strength from within, and put a fearless
trust in the message that it bears.

*September* 22, 1868.

LONDON: PRINTED BY W. CLOWES AND SONS, DUKE STREET, STAMFORD STREET,
AND CHARING CROSS.